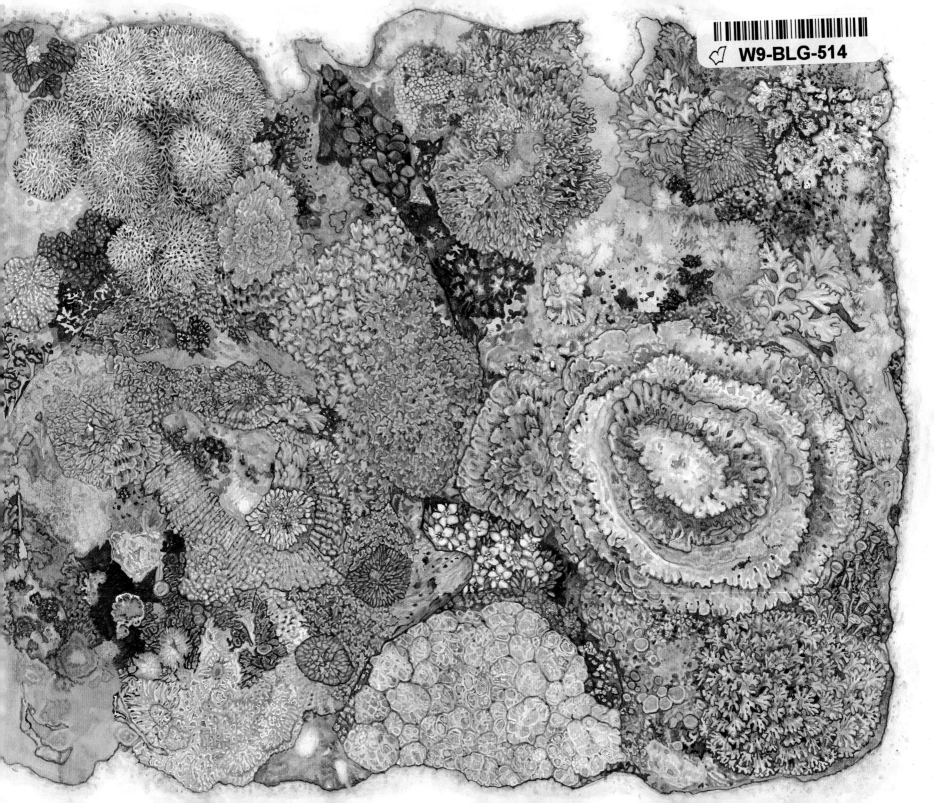

JAN BRETT
COZY

putnam

G. P. PUTNAM'S SONS

For Lia, Tom, Torynn, and Brian Koloski,
my Alaskan family

Thank you to Mark Austin and friends at the Musk Ox Farm in Palmer, Alaska

G. P. PUTNAM'S SONS
An imprint of Penguin Random House LLC, New York

Copyright © 2020 by Jan Brett

Visit us online at penguinrandomhouse.com

Library of Congress Cataloging-in-Publication Data
Names: Brett, Jan, 1949- author, illustrator.
Title: Cozy / Jan Brett.
Description: New York: G. P. Putnam's Sons, [2020] | Summary: The coat of a huge woolly musk ox named Cozy
is the winter home for a growing number of Alaskan animals who mostly get along.
Identifiers: LCCN 2019039708 (print) | LCCN 2019039709 (ebook) | ISBN 9780593109793 (hardcover) |
ISBN 9780593109816 (kindle edition) | ISBN 9780593109809 (ebook)
Subjects: CYAC: Muskox—Fiction. | Animals—Alaska—Fiction. | Winter—Fiction. | Alaska—Fiction.
Classification: LCC PZ7.B7559 Cr 2020 (print) | LCC PZ7.B7559 (ebook) | DDC [E]—dc23
LC record available at https://lccn.loc.gov/2019039708
LC ebook record available at https://lccn.loc.gov/2019039709

Manufactured in China by RR Donnelley Asia Printing Solutions Ltd.
ISBN 9780593109793
1 3 5 7 9 10 8 6 4 2

Design by Marikka Tamura | Text set in Worcester Round Medium
The art for the book was done in watercolor and gouache
Airbrush backgrounds by Joseph Hearne

Storms rolled over the tundra when Cozy the musk ox was separated from his herd. He was used to being with his family. His mother and father had named him Cozy because his silky coat was so soft and thick.

Cozy braced himself against the wind, and his thick coat warmed him like a blanket.

In a tussock, a mother lemming's pups were squeaking loudly.
"I'm cold! I'm cold! I'm cold!" She used a triple carry to tunnel them
toward a new spot, where she saw a towering mountain of fur.

In no time, the lemming family settled in next to Cozy's left hoof.

"Shh . . . ," she whispered. "Quiet voices, and that musk ox will never notice us."

Snowshoe Hare, feeling chilly, had the same idea.
"Master Musk Ox," he asked politely, "may I wait out
the storm under the protection of your very thick coat?"

Cozy was happy for the company and well aware that a lemming family had snuck in. He said, "Welcome, Snowshoe Hare. But mind those lemmings—quiet voices and gentle thumping only."

Snow swirled and—
phlump—suddenly
all grew white.

Was it a clump of snow that had hit
Cozy on the forehead? No, it was feathers.
When Cozy opened his eyes, he was
looking into big yellow ones.

The eyes belonged to a snowy owl, who also had a request. "Oh, magnificent Oomingmak, would you be so kind as to give me shelter? The wind has tumbled me terribly."

Cozy knew that snowy owls and lemmings and snowshoe hares
were not always fast friends. But he agreed, with some conditions.
"House rules are quiet voices, gentle thumping, claws to yourself."

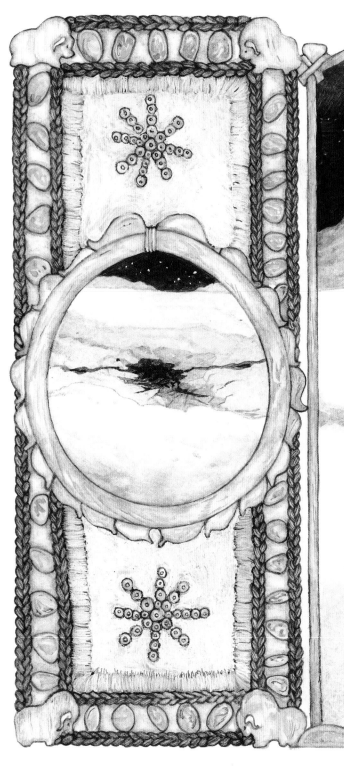

Arctic Fox's nose was turning blue. Her bushy tail wasn't warm enough, and every time she wrapped it around herself, the wind unwrapped it.

Thinking Cozy would make a good windbreak, she sidled up to him. "Do you mind, Mr. Musk Ox, if I unfreeze my nose in your thick fluff?"

Cozy was happy to welcome
a new guest, but eyeing her sharp canines,
he answered, "For the harmony of all, quiet voices,
gentle thumping, claws to yourself, and no biting."

As winter went by, the storms grew worse. The wind blew and blew, and a low humpy shape appeared, swaying and shuffling. Its coat was covered with ice balls.

"Shaggy beast," it growled, "I fell into an ice floe and am chilled to the bone. Can you help me?"

Cozy was happy to invite the wolverine in, but added to the house rules. "Quiet voices, gentle thumping, claws to yourself, no biting, and no pouncing."

Cozy's new friends cleaned their coats, preened their feathers, napped, and were glad for their comfy shelter.

But then, above the wind, the animals heard, "Yip! Yip! Yip!"

A team of huskies, always on the lookout for a good thing, barreled into Cozy's big bulk, flinging the creatures in all directions.

Their musher, a sea otter, looked on in dismay.

"Hi." The lead dog grinned.

"House rules!" chorused the jostled lemmings, snowshoe hare, snowy owl, arctic fox, and wolverine. "Quiet voices, gentle thumping, claws to yourself, no biting, no pouncing, and be mindful of others!"

Cozy, wary of the lead dog, who looked a lot like a wolf, shook, shook, shook his horns to make sure the huskies understood.

As time went by, the wind calmed a little and the Arctic sun
climbed higher in the sky. The animals felt more at home every day.
But Cozy had spring fever. "I want to find my family.
How can I move about with these visitors underfoot?"

The house rules were stretched every day. When was a nibble a bite?
When was a hoot quiet or loud?

There was bumping, making faces, and nobody was saying,
"I'm sorry."

One sunny day, the lemmings were playing climb the ladder.
A great chunk of Cozy's coat came off. Then another hank
came off in Snowy Owl's talons.

Cozy remembered this from last year. Shedding meant
it was finally spring in Alaska.

Hank by hank, all of Cozy's warm, silky winter coat
drifted down the slope.

Cozy's lodgers started heading to their spring homes.
Cozy hadn't felt so free and breezy since he was a calf.
He jumped. He gamboled.

And then, in the middle
of a gleeful leap, he saw
his herd.

He ran to join his mother, his father, his sister, and his brother.

"Where were you? We were worried!" said his sister, Fluffy.

"We missed you!" said his brother, Snuggly.
"I made some new friends," Cozy told them.
But it was nice to get back to musk ox ways.

They all formed a circle, babies in the middle. But Cozy felt curiously alone.

Then the breeze carried squeaky and growly and whistling voices. "See you next year, Cozy!"

"Meet you when the snow flies, Cozy!"

The snowshoe hare thump, thump, thumped as they all called, "We can't wait to get cozy with Cozy!"

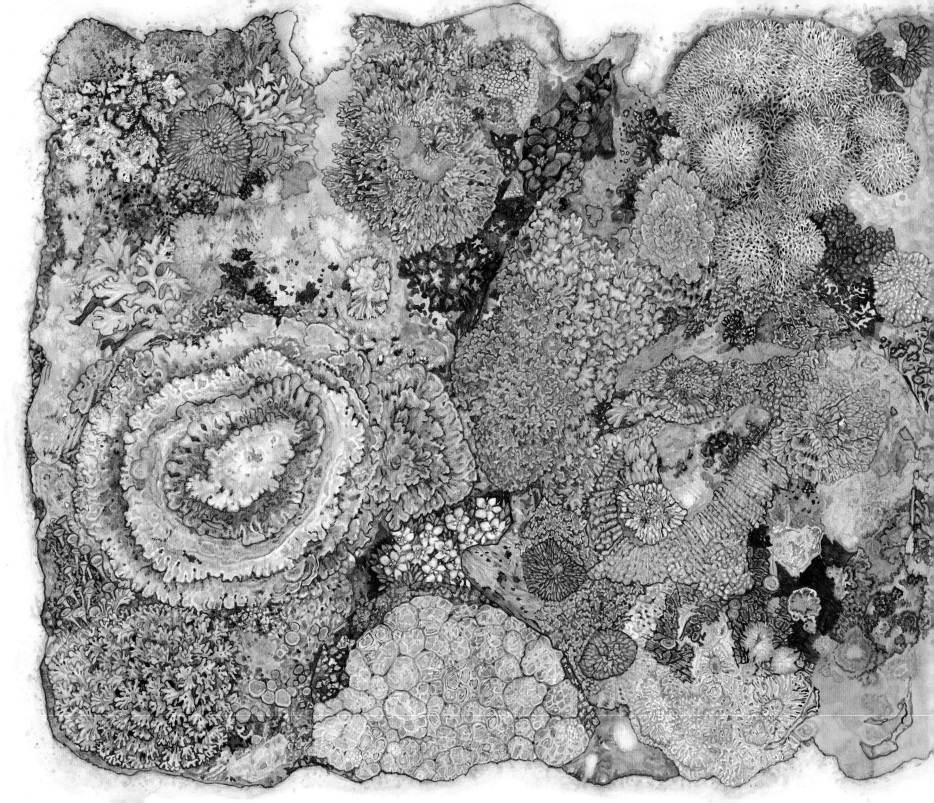